Noir Pointblank

by David Landau

Music and Lyrics by
Nikki Stern

A SAMUEL FRENCH ACTING EDITION

SAMUEL
FRENCH

FOUNDED 1830

SAMUELFRENCH.COM

ISBN 978-0-573-69965-8   Printed in U.S.A.   #28004

RENTAL MATERIALS

A CD consisting of **rehearsal and performance backing tracks** will be loaned two months prior to the production ONLY on the receipt of the Licensing Fee quoted for all performances, the rental fee and a refundable deposit.

Please contact Samuel French for perusal of the music materials as well as a performance license application.

IMPORTANT BILLING AND CREDIT REQUIREMENTS

All producers of *NOIR POINTBLANK* *must* give credit to the Authors of the Play in all programs distributed in connection with performances of the Play, and in all instances in which the title of the Play appears for the purposes of advertising, publicizing or otherwise exploiting the Play and/ or a production. The name of the Authors *must* appear on a separate line on which no other name appears, immediately following the title and *must* appear in size of type not less than fifty percent of the size of the title type.

NOIR POINTBLANK first opened at the Murder To Go Dinner Theater in Cedar Knolls, New Jersey January 8, 1994. The cast was as follows:

RICH ARCHER	David Flynn
ANTHONY CAIRO	Joe Prussak
MAUREEN TEMPLE/SHEILA WONDERLY	Tricia Burr
EDWARD STEINBERG/BEN TEMPLE	Michael Mooney
SYDNEY TREVOR	Shelly Matiss
JEAN DIJON/SGT. INSTONE	Michelle Begley
SAM LYRIC	Bill Chermerka

CHARACTERS

(in order of appearance)

RICK ARCHER - ex-PI, owner of the Cafe Noir

ANTHONY CAIRO - a dealer in the blackmarket on the run.

MAUREEN TEMPLE - a British hit woman.

EDWARD G. STEINBERG - a New York gangster on the lam in Mustique.

SYDNEY TREVOR - an American woman, nightclub singer

JEAN DIJON - a French art historian

BEN TEMPLE - a British mob lawyer and Maureen's brother (same actor as Edward G.)

DT. SAM LYRIC - an NYPD Detective, looking for Maureen

SGT. JOANNE INSTONE - the Mustique constable assigned to escort Sam (same actress as Jean)

SHEILA WONDERLY - ex-call girl and co-owner of the Cafe Noir (same actress as Maureen)

INSPECTOR RIGFIELD - St. Vincent police (same actor as Edward G.)

SETTING

The Cafe Noir, where everything and everyone is in black, white or grey. Hung around the room are old photos and etchings of Mustique Island's past 300 years. The display includes etchings of pirates, photos of German U-boats, a sea monster, 40's era bathing beauties, and various nefarious looking people. A sign in the room reads "Cafe Noir salutes Mustique Island, 300 yrs of shady business."

AUTHOR'S NOTES

As patrons arrive, they are given a program laid out as a passport. Inside is a sleuth sheet asking: Whodunit? Whydunit? What famous movie inspired this play (there are eight obvious references to this movie in the show)?

SCENE 1

(As guests arrive they are seated by **RICK**, **CAIRO**, *and* **SYDNEY**. **JEAN** *and* **STEINBERG** *are looking over the display. On the tables are newspapers with a headline "Mob Silences Squealers" and a smaller article about Mustique Island's 300th birthday [see newspaper provided]. Theme music plays. Lights dim out. A spot light comes up on* **RICK**.*)*

RICK. Have you ever found yourself in a position to help someone who really needs your help, and knows it, but would rather not have any help at all? Sure you have. Who hasn't? But sometimes it's not as simple as ego, or self-determination on the help worthy part. Sometimes it's something deeper, something clouded over and shaded in. Sometimes the truth is they're afraid that with help, they'll actually succeed and that's the outcome they want to avoid at all costs.

Right now you're probably asking yourself, what the hell is this guy talking about? Well, I'm going to help you out with that. My handle is Richard Archer, but everyone calls me just plain Rick. I'm an ex-private eye from San Francisco who took a case that landed me on some small time forgotten island in the eastern Caribbean called Mustique. It was a tropical island that drifted right out of a black and white Bogie movie. In other words it felt like home. So I stayed and became the co-owner and manager of a little supper club called the Cafe Noir.

(Lights up. **RICK** *walks around, gesturing to patrons, etc.)*

RICK. Okay, so maybe the patrons weren't exactly the cream of the crop. But they always paid their debts, and I don't mean just to the Cafe. You might say they were the kind of people you would catch dead. They did dirty jobs, but someone had to feed them and the Cafe Noir did that and more. As the previous manager said, it was a place where the dishonest could be honest about it. There was a secret behind every pair of eyes, a threat between every pair of lips, a dubious deal under every breath. Maybe there was something in the air of this dockside bistro wedged between century old warehouses. Maybe it was the delicate mixture of the sea spray, the musty smells and the toxic breath of some of the regulars that made Cafe Noir a fateful port in the storm for so many lost excursions. Then again, maybe it was just bad luck. But I'm getting poetic, and that's not what I set out to tell you. Or maybe it is – I'll let you be the judge of that.

It all started when gambling casinos starting opening up on the nearby island of Tobago Cay. The sudden popularity of the area made the property values skyrocket, along with the taxes, cafe licenses and every other cost of doing business. And it made us behind in our mortgage payments.

(CAIRO brings a few letters and a newspaper up to RICK. CAIRO looks at the sign and then around at the display.)

CAIRO. Do you really think this display will bring in more business, Mr. Rick?

RICK. Sure. It has already.

(RICK motions to a table of patrons. CAIRO and RICK both look disappointed.)

RICK. Okay, maybe it's not the best we could hope for, but at least the chairs aren't empty.

CAIRO. That may be a matter of opinion.

RICK. Well, it has gotten us some press, even in the states and it's cheaper than hiring that singer you talked me into hiring.

(RICK looks over towards SYDNEY at the bar. She smiles at them. They both smile back.)

CAIRO. But less attractive.

RICK. True. I'm glad you're back out of prison, Cairo. Do you think you can catch up on our books before you make a return engagement?

CAIRO. No problem, Mr. Rick. Out of curiosity, how did you find out this year is Mustique's 300th birthday?

RICK. I didn't. But I'm sure it's at least that old. At least the plumbing in this place seems to be. Did you ever call the plumber?

CAIRO. Yeah, they said they'll send someone right over.

(As CAIRO nods, MAUREEN, sexy in appearance and wearing sunglasses, enters and stops to look about. RICK and CAIRO look at her.)

CAIRO & RICK. Nawh.

(RICK approaches her.)

RICK. Good evening Madam, and welcome to the Cafe Noir. I'm this evening's manager, Rick Archer, and if there is anything I can do for you – which I'm sure men say to you all the time.

MAUREEN. Charming, Mr. Archer, but –

RICK. You can call me just plain Rick.

MAUREEN. Alright, Mr. Just Plain Rick, but I'm here to meet someone.

RICK. That's all there really is to life when it comes down to it. May I get you a drink?

MAUREEN. I hear there's a house specialty, a Maltese Falcon?

(RICK nods and exits to bar. MAUREEN sees STEINBERG by a photo of a German U-Boat sinking, obviously taken at dusk. She approaches him.)

STEINBERG. *(still looking at photos)* The Atlantic was the hunting ground for the German wolf packs. Do you have any idea how many U-boats came past here during the war?

MAUREEN. I can't say that I have, nor do I care.

STEINBERG. It's just that torpedoes always seem to fancy these waters.

MAUREEN. Maybe it's a good place to hit their targets from. Have you seen the latest paper from the states?

(**MAUREEN** *hands him the paper.* **STEINBERG** *smiles as he reads it.*)

MAUREEN. You know, England courts my fancy this time of year. After I collect the balance due on some unsettled business, I think I'll be heading back to London.

STEINBERG. Then perhaps you'll need a little extra spending money.

(**STEINBERG** *hands her a grey envelope full of bills.* **MAUREEN** *pulls a $1,000 bill out and examines its mint condition.*)

MAUREEN. Madison, my favorite American.

(*She puts the envelope in her purse.*)

STEINBERG. You're not going to count all ten of them?

MAUREEN. You wouldn't shortchange me. No one's that foolish.

STEINBERG. Leaving soon?

MAUREEN. Tomorrow. And yourself?

STEINBERG. (*turning back to the photos*) I have a personal interest in something down here. It started out as just a hobby, but now it's become almost an obsession.

MAUREEN. Fishing or diving?

STEINBERG. A little of both. Now that our business dealings are concluded, perhaps we could –

MAUREEN. No thank you, Mr. Steinberg. As I told you before, I never get social with a client.

STEINBERG. Such a pity. Have a safe flight, Ms. Temple.

MAUREEN. I always do, Mr. Steinberg. I always do.

(*As she leaves him he looks after her lustfully, then exits. Across the room,* **SYDNEY** *is looking at a photo of the Mustique police force from the turn of the century.* **CAIRO** *nervously walks up.*)

CAIRO. I think they're all retired.

SYDNEY. You would know, wouldn't you, Cairo?

CAIRO. I lived up to my part of the bargain, Sydney. He's right over there. *(looks off to where* **STEINBERG** *was)* Well, he was over there.

SYDNEY. Yes, I saw him. Thank you, Cairo.

(She hands him an airplane ticket.)

CAIRO. Your passport?

SYDNEY. I never agreed to that. Just to help you fly.

CAIRO. But I need a passport! Sydney's a man's name. Look, I even have the photo already.

*(***CAIRO*** pulls out a passport size photo of himself. It's obviously a mug shot with the numbers cut off the bottom.* **SYDNEY** *finds it a little humorous.)*

SYDNEY. My husband always said you were a resourceful man. I'm sure you'll come up with something. Staying for dinner?

CAIRO. I was hoping to be off this island by then.

*(***CAIRO*** starts in the direction* **STEINBERG** *was in last, but stops behind* **JEAN**, *who is looking over some photos of seaplanes and beautiful girls in shorts.)*

CAIRO. *(picking up girlie photo)* This island's always been a favorite for migrating birds.

JEAN. Trappers – they were women employed by British intelligence to intercept documents from travelers whose plane or ship stopped here to refuel.

*(***CAIRO*** sees the reports.)*

CAIRO. They also intercepted radio signals here as well. Looks like a busy night for this gal. A refueling vessel got lost in the reefs and an SOS signal from a submarine – an ERR sub –

JEAN. *(interrupting)* This was a natural site selection as both planes and ships had to refuel somewhere in the mid-Atlantic. Though officially under British rule the French population provided the Vishy a base to refuel the roving U-boats. Dijon's the name, Jean Dijon.

I'm a historian doing some research for a new book. Fascinating place, your Mustique.

CAIRO. Some fascinating rumors about what was refueled here as well, considering we're sort of on the way between Europe and South America.

(JEAN becomes very interested, leaning in close.)

JEAN. Are they more than just rumors?

CAIRO. Is the Statue of Liberty still in New York harbor?

JEAN. *(not realizing CAIRO is being facetious)* Yes, I think so.

CAIRO. Perhaps, we can help each other out. You see, I'm having a bit of an identity crisis – I seem to have lost my passport. Now, as Jean is spelled the same as the man's name Jean, you could loan me your passport and tomorrow afternoon you could report it missing – after my plane's taken off, of course. You'd have no problem getting a new one from the French consulate. And I could pay you five hundred dollars for your troubles.

JEAN. You want to leave Mustique?

CAIRO. There comes a time when a man must move on. Let's say the sooner I leave, the better for my health. I'm an expert on the waters down here. Did you know that there is only one way through the reefs surrounding Mustique?

JEAN. And you're a man who knows the ins and outs?

CAIRO. *(pausing over the sexual innuendo)* I know the rumors. I could help you become the most famous historian in history. That is if what you think is down there – is down there. Personally, I don't care what's down there. But I know where there is, and I can get you down to it. All you have to do is help me see Liberty.

JEAN. This is a very tempting proposition, Mr. – ?

CAIRO. Cairo. Anthony Cairo, at your service.

JEAN. Very tempting. If you'll pardon me while I give it due consideration?

(CAIRO nods, and JEAN exits in thought. CAIRO looks back at the report and toasts it with his drink.)

CAIRO. You, my dear Adolph, may be my ticket out of here.

(BEN *intercepts* RICK *on his way to* MAUREEN *with a drink.*)

BEN. Mr. Archer, isn't it?

RICK. The last time I checked. But everyone seems to call me just plain Rick. Here for the exhibit?

BEN. In a way, Rick. I heard you were experiencing some financial difficulties.

RICK. Who told you that? *(to audience member)* Did you tell him that?

BEN. Temple's the name, Ben Temple. And perhaps you might be able to use some extra cash.

RICK. Perhaps is an understatement, Mr. Temple.

BEN. Then you might be just the man I'm looking for, to join a small expedition – one that could yield quite a little profit.

RICK. How little?

BEN. It could be quite sizable, and then it could prove to be just an exercise in nocturnal diving. It'll only take tonight to determine which.

RICK. You want to go diving? Tonight?

BEN. We have to act fast, lest someone beats us to it.

RICK. The Caribbean certainly has beautiful crystal blue water. But that's during the day. It gets pretty dark down there at night, Mr. Temple. Dark like the inside of a mausoleum. You'll need underwater lights, an extra generator, not to mention the usual –

BEN. But you Americans are known for your resourcefulness. Would one thousand American dollars help you?

(BEN *begins to pull some money out of his pocket – then freezes as* RICK *turns to the audience.*)

RICK. Would it? Okay folks, if you were in my shoes, what would you do? We're so far behind on our mortgage the bank's trying to find some sucker to take it off their hands. Now, I don't know this joker from a three card monte dealer. Who's to say what he wants me to do is even legal? Then again, I'm just a hired hand, supplying a few supplies which wouldn't be too hard to collect. By a show of hands, how many say I should steer clear of this shadowy diving? *(audience votes)* Okay, and how many say take the chance and the thousand bucks? *(audience votes)*

VERSION A – TO TAKE THE JOB

(BEN begins to recount his money.)

BEN. Now, now, Mr. Rick. I'm sure you could find a good use for a small portrait of your president Madison.

RICK. I'm sure I could. I could hang it in the back room between Millard Fillmore and Calvin Coolidge. But, if you'd prefer, you don't have to risk that much. How about five hundred down, and ten percent of whatever we find?

BEN. *(putting money away)* You Americans are also known for your quick business sense. Very well, Mr. Archer, ten percent. You could find yourself with as much as a hundred thousand dollars.

RICK. I'm not sure what it is you think is down there, but keep thinking it. Maybe it'll show up out of obligation. It'll only take me about an hour to round up the gear, charts –

BEN. Don't worry about the charts. I already have what we'll need.

RICK. Fine. I'll meet you on the dock behind the cafe in an hour. Oh, and don't forget the little matter of that cash advance.

BEN. You'll have your five hundred before we sail, Mr. Archer. I'm sure this will prove to be a short, but profitable friendship.

RICK. Let's hope we can bank on it. Why don't you buy yourself a drink at the bar –

(BEN takes RICK's drink.)

BEN. No, thank you. I already have one. And as far as that boat – well, as I mentioned, time is of the utmost importance, just plain Rick.

(BEN takes a sip. RICK exits. MAUREEN joins BEN.)

VERSION B – NOT TO TAKE THE JOB

(**BEN** *begins to recount his money.*)

BEN. Now, now, Mr. Rick. I'm sure you could find a good use for a small portrait of your president Madison.

RICK. I'm sure I could. I could hang it in the back room between Millard Fillmore and Calvin Coolidge. But, right now I've got to get to work.

BEN. *(putting money away)* You Americans are also known for your quick bargining sense. Very well, Mr. Archer, ten percent of whatever we find. You could find yourself with as much as a hundred thousand dollars.

RICK. I'm not sure what it is you think is down there, but keep thinking it. Maybe it'll show up out of obligation. Where at this time of night do you think you can round up the gear, charts –

BEN. Don't worry about the charts. I already have what we'll need.

RICK. You mean what you'll need.

BEN. I'll meet you on the dock behind the cafe in an hour. I'll give you a five hundred deposit before we sail, Mr. Archer. I'm sure this will prove to be a short, but profitable friendship.

RICK. I'll think about it. Why don't you buy yourself a drink at the bar?

(**BEN** *takes* **RICK**'s *drink.*)

BEN. No, thank you. I already have one. And as far as that boat – well, as I mentioned, time is of the utmost importance, just plain Rick.

(**BEN** *takes a sip.* **RICK** *exits.* **MAUREEN** *joins Ben.*)

BOTH VERSIONS CONTINUE

BEN. Paid in full, Love?

MAUREEN. Of course. Shall we fly?

BEN. I was thinking, we might stay the weekend. I've happened onto something that might be worth our diving into. Something people have been looking for since 1945 and your Mr. Steinberg helped tune me in to.

MAUREEN. The heat must have gotten to you, love.

BEN. No. It's this exhibit. That's why Steinberg's staying on.

MAUREEN. Steinberg's staying on here til the heat cools down in the States, Love. He's bought property and changed his citizenship, to make extrication by the US as difficult as possible.

BEN. He's a smart one, your Mr. Steinberg.

MAUREEN. Please, Ben darling. He's only a client. I certainly don't have low enough taste to make him mine. *(looks at him)* You know, I never noticed this before, but you look a bit like –

BEN. I'm one step ahead of Steinberg though. I've lined up a boat and some diving gear for tonight.

MAUREEN. Tonight? You're bloody balmy.

BEN. Come on, Love. You're the one who said we should take full advantage of our short stay here. And you did so want to go diving.

MAUREEN. Not at night.

BEN. But I've already arranged things with Mr. Archer, the Cafe's manager. Come on, it'll sound much better after another drink. I'll freshen you up.

(BEN takes her drink and heads for the bar. DT. SAM LYRIC, dressed in a rumpled trenchcoat, enters with JOANNE.)

JOANNE. If this hit-woman you're looking for is anywhere on these islands, you'll find her here, Detective, at the Cafe Noir. It attracts the dregs of island society. *(to female audience member)* She's a regular pinup for vice, *(to male audience member)* and this guy's been in the holding pen so often his toothbrush and striped pajamas are under the pillow.

*(**CAIRO** sees **JOANNE** and tries to sneak out.)*

JOANNE. Mr. Cairo! Back at work at the Cafe Noir? The only place I've ever seen you without a pair of handcuffs on.

CAIRO. We all have to make a living, Sergeant Instone.

JOANNE. You have to testify as a prosecution witness. You wouldn't be thinking of leaving the island, would you, Mr. Cairo?

CAIRO. Why would anyone want to leave lovely Mustique?

JOANNE. *(pinching **CAIRO**'s cheek)* You're so cute, Cairo. We're watching you. You make one wrong move and you'll be in hard labor for twenty years.

CAIRO. Just because I sailed a boat into harbor without notifying customs? Isn't a man entitled to a simple mistake?

JOANNE. Your mistake was carrying a cargo of stolen jewelry and electronic goods and trying to sell it to undercover agents.

CAIRO. Now, how was I supposed to know it was stolen? I'm just a small businessman –

JOANNE. Well you can stop giving me the business, because I'm not buying.

CAIRO. *(whispered)* If I go on the stand, I'm a dead man.

JOANNE. You should have thought of that before you started your importing business. Where's Rick and Sheila?

CAIRO. Ms. Wonderly is in Barbados visiting her mother. She should be back tomorrow. Mr. Rick is right – well he was right here a moment ago.

*(**SAM** has walked up behind **MAUREEN** and takes a firm hold of her arm.)*

SAM. Hello there, Laura.

MAUREEN. Maureen – Maureen Temple and please unhand me.

(She tries to pull free, but **SAM** *tightens his grip.)*

SAM. Funny, it was Laura Mason just the other night in New York. You remember, the night Samuel Rocco of the harbor Commission was pumped full of .357 magnum slugs. Rocco, the man we persuaded to turn evidence against his mobster buddies. Or perhaps you remember the five evenings before that? The ones spent at the theater, at that little French place in the village, or in my double post bed.

MAUREEN. You're bloody crazy. I've never seen you before in my life. *(To* **JOANNE***)* Officer, make this man release me at once.

*(***SAM*** releases her as* **JOANNE** *joins them.)*

JOANNE. I hope you know what you're doing.

SAM. I certainly do, and so does she.

BEN. *(coming up with drinks)* What seems to be the matter?

SAM. None of your business, fellah. Sergeant, if we can get those extradition papers out of the way, I'll be leaving for New York with my prisoner.

JOANNE. It's not going to be as easy as all that, Sam.

BEN. It certainly is not. I happen to be this woman's legal counsel. What in the world are you alleging, sir?

SAM. Legal counsel? That's proof right there, Joanne. Nobody honest goes out with a lawyer.

JOANNE. Detective Lyric is here from the New York City police, trying to locate a certain woman they believe to have assassinated one of their corrupt politicians.

SAM. I wish you wouldn't make it sound so commonplace.

BEN. Well, it just so happens that this woman is my sister and we've been here in Mustique for the past two weeks. You have identification, I assume?

*(***JOANNE*** shows* **BEN** *her badge.* **BEN** *stares at* **SAM***, who then shows him his badge.)*

SAM. This is all a crock of bull. Last week, that woman was warming the other side of my bed so she could get a clear shot at Rocco.

BEN. Libel and defamation of character are only two of the charges we are prepared to file. Of course we'll file for a suspension of any extrication pending a court decision on the validity of any alleged evidence.

MAUREEN. As well as a psychiatric review of this officer's competency. The man is a positive loon!

JOANNE. Sam, are you sure you're not acting hastily?

SAM. Joanne, unfortunately I do not have so many women passing through my bedroom that I could confuse their faces.

BEN. We are British citizens and you have no authority over us whatsoever. Sergeant, I will demand an audience with the police commissioner tomorrow morning.

SAM. Great! We can all go together. Maybe I can pin something on you too and make it a double header.

JOANNE. Give me a break, Sam. Tomorrow morning we'll all go before police commissioner John Houston and let him decide. I'm afraid I'll have to order the two of you not to leave the island. And you better be right, Sam, because if you're jumping the gun –

SAM. Shooting her would have been jumping the gun.

JOANNE. Sam, I'm afraid I must strongly suggest you go for a walk and cool yourself down.

(**SAM** *is about to say "no," then storms out.*)

MAUREEN. Thank you, officer.

JOANNE. Where are you staying?

BEN. The Blue Parrot on Tobago Cay. We'll stay as long as required, Officer. Thank you for you assistance. May we buy you – a drink?

JOANNE. No. But it looks like you've already bought yourself some time. Don't do anything illegal with it. Cairo, how does someone get a bite to eat around here?

(**CAIRO** *claps his hands, the first course is served.*)

(**CAIRO** *steals the two photos of the German U-boat, hiding them inside his jacket as he exits. He goes from table to table offering to buy people's passports.*)

(**BEN** *steals the report of the ERR submarine.*)

SCENE II

(Music intro. A few gunshots ring out. **MAUREEN** *staggers in, shot, holding a gun. She fires back out the door at her assailant. As she collapses,* **SAM** *runs in, gun drawn. He goes to her.)*

SAM. You've got one last chance now of setting things straight. You can't tell me these past five days were all an act.

MAUREEN. *(dying)* Cute, Sam, real cute. You watched too many of those movies when you were a kid. *(coughs)* What do you expect me to do? Make a dying confession? Tell you I loved you?

*(***RICK*** *runs in, bumping into* **SAM**, *who drops* **MAUREEN**. *They both look down at her.)*

BOTH. Oops.

RICK. Her lawyer brother's dead on a boat at the dock just outside.

SAM. *(to* **RICK***)* Okay, up against the wall, fellah!

*(***SAM*** *throws* **RICK** *against a wall and handcuffs him.* **SAM** *goes to* **MAUREEN** *who is barely alive.* **JOANNE** *comes dashing in and goes to* **MAUREEN**.*)*

JOANNE. Would you like to make a statement?

SAM. *(to* **MAUREEN***)* You look like you're about to be fish food. There's no honor among murderers – don't be a fool. Who hired you, who pulled the trigger? Come on – you bought the farm, grabbed a cab, bit the dust, knocking on the gates, dancing with the angels –

MAUREEN. I get the message – *(cough)*

SAM. Not talking, huh? Maybe this will convince you.

(Music starts. **SAM** *(or* **RICK***) sings* **COME CLEAN**. *Throughout the song,* **MAUREEN** *continues trying to confess and tell who hired her, but* **SAM** *keeps singing instead of listening to her. During the first verse, everyone enters.)*

SAM.

YOUR DAYS ARE NUMBERED
YOU'VE BEEN SHOT THROUGH THE HEART

> YOU WANNA BARE YOUR SOUL
> BEFORE YOU DEPART?
> WE CAN DO THIS THE HARD WAY
> YOU KNOW WHAT I MEAN
> OR YOU CAN COME CLEAN

CHORUS.

> COME CLEAN

MAUREEN. You're right, I –

RICK.

> SO WHY CLAM UP
> AND TAKE THE SECRET TO YOUR GRAVE
> FINGER THE FINK
> THINK OF THE TROUBLE YOU'LL SAVE
> DON'T HOLD OUT ON US, SISTER
> SPILL THE BEANS
> LADY, COME CLEAN

MAUREEN. Okay, I'll tell you. It –

CHORUS.

> COME CLEAN WHILE YOU CAN
> AND TAKE A LOAD OFF YOUR CHEST

RICK.

> YOU CLUE US IN
> AND WE'LL TAKE CARE OF THE REST

CHORUS.

> COME CLEAN AND YOUR CONSCIENCE
> WILL FINALLY BE FREE

SAM.

> SPEAK YOUR PEACE
> CLEAR THE AIR
> YOU CAN SHARE IT WITH ME
> COME CLEAN

MAUREEN. I'm trying to tell you it was –

RICK.

> JUST BLOW THE WHISTLE
> DROP A DIME ON THE GUY
> WE'LL GO INVESTIGATE
> AS SOON AS YOU DIE

YOU CAN RAT ON THE LOUSE
TELL US ALL WHAT YOU SEEN
YOU CAN COME CLEAN

CHORUS.

COME CLEAN

MAUREEN. Alright, I –

SAM.

SO PUT US WISE
AND YOU CAN SING LIKE A BIRD
YOU WANNA SOUND OFF
WE'LL MAKE SURE THAT YOU'RE HEARD
SPIT IT OUT
COUGH IT UP
SPILL YOUR GUTS
OR YOUR SPLEEN
COME ON, COME CLEAN

MAUREEN. You're not making this easy –

CHORUS.

COME CLEAN
YOU CAN LET THE CAT OUT OF THE BAG

RICK.

WHY NOT CONFESS
BEFORE YOUR TOE WEARS A TAG
WHO'RE YOU PROTECTING
TELL US
WHAT DOES IT MEAN

JOANNE.

YOU GOTTA FESS UP

RICK.

UNLOAD

CAIRO.

TIP YOUR HAND

STEINBERG.

BLOW THE GAFF

SYDNEY.

DISH THE DIRT

MAUREEN. Will you all shut up?

SAM & CHORUS.

COME CLEAN

(By the end of the song, which everyone has joined in singing, she dies.)

CAIRO. Maybe we shouldn't have sung that last verse.

RICK. And I never even got my cash advance.

JOANNE. Detective, I'll take that weapon, please. And take the cuffs off this man.

RICK. Don't worry, I won't die on you. Not if I have any say in the matter.

*(**SAM** hands the gun over to **JOANNE**. As **JOANNE** smells the gun, he releases **RICK**.)*

JOANNE. It's been fired.

SAM. Someone fired at me – I fired back. All I hit was a couple of coconuts.

RICK. He almost hit me.

SAM. You were running away.

RICK. I don't run towards gunshots, like some people around here.

SAM. Who are you?

JOANNE. This is Richard Archer, an ex-private eye from the states and the manager of the Cafe Noir. But everyone calls him just plain Rick.

RICK. Officer, you wouldn't mind if we move this corpse to the back room, would you? I don't think the St. Vincent health officials would okay this as a menu selection.

(She nods.)

RICK. Mr. Cairo will be happy to lend you some assistance, officer.

*(**CAIRO** reluctantly comes forward. **JOANNE** reluctantly helps **CAIRO** remove the corpse.)*

SAM. Okay, just plain Rick, where were you running off to in such a hurry?

RICK. Someplace where the air is reserved for birds. Bullets and I don't get along. *(calling after them)* And watch her –

(There is a loud crash.)

RICK. – head.

SAM. Perhaps you can explain how you ended up on board a boat with two corpses?

RICK. One of the corpses wanted to hire me and the boat to go diving this evening.

JOANNE. *(coming back in)* Diving – where, for what?

RICK. Ask the corpse – he never told me.

SAM. How is it that you ended up without so much as a broken nail?

RICK. I was coming up from below with some more supplies for the cafe when I heard gunshots coming from at least three directions. The next thing I know Ben Temple is dead at the bow and this woman is running towards the boat with a gun. I decided not to stick around and find out what her complaint was. I sprinted to the cafe's back door, then you shot at me so I dove for cover behind the dumpster. When it sounded like the coast was clear I came in here and was treated to the sight of you running lines from a Bogart/Bacall movie.

SAM. Smart guy, huh? Well, I better go check out that boat –

JOANNE. Your work is finished here, Sam. Your suspect is dead, and this murder investigation is a matter for the St. Vincent police. Unfortunately, I'll have to order you to stay on the island, as you are now a suspect.

SAM. ME?

RICK. It's not so bad, being a suspect. Why, everyone in this place is suspected of something. *(pats an audience member)* Some more than others. Now you fit right in.

SAM. Thanks all the same, Mr. Just Plain Rick, but –

JOANNE. I have to go make a report to headquarters. Mustique falls under Inspector Rigfield's territory.

RICK. Good old Rigfield, made full inspector at last huh? How'd he do it?

JOANNE. You can ask him yourself when he gets down here. *(to Sam)* You're just a civilian now, Sam. For your own good, you better start acting that way.

(JOANNE exits. SAM is mad.)

SAM. This'll look just great to my police commissioner back in the States. And it sure puts me in a hell of a jam, stuck here until they solve this thing.

RICK. Well, maybe I can help you out, by helping pinpoint who killed her.

SAM. You? Buy yourself another drink, Humphrey Bogart. At least she deserved it. Whoever did her in gets my envy. And you, Mr. Just Plain Rick, should keep to your own business and let the police handle theirs.

RICK. Sure. But a corpse in my club might start to give the place a bad reputation. People might think it was the service or something. So you might say it is my business to prove it otherwise.

SYDNEY. Some photos are missing.

RICK. Pardon?

SYDNEY. Two of the pictures are missing. They were here before the first course, but now they're gone.

RICK. Do you remember what they were of? Anyone remember?

(Someone will remember submarines; even if not –)

STEINBERG. This is just terrible. After you've gone and collected all these irreplaceable photos. Unless they're not the originals?

RICK. I'm afraid they are. Which ones walked?

STEINBERG. One was of a U-boat, I think. I don't remember the other. Where was it you were going to take them? The two deceased, that is.

RICK. They didn't say. He said he had a chart already.

STEINBERG. Did he bring the chart to the boat?

RICK. I don't remember seeing it. Why are you so interested, Mr – ?

STEINBERG. Steinberg, Edward G. Steinberg. Two photos vanish – two corpses appear. I think it's a bit more than coincidence.

RICK. I wouldn't think it's worth killing over.

STEINBERG. But photos can lead you to many things. Somebody obviously felt it was worth more than a few lives. How much did he say he would pay you?

RICK. Five hundred dollars.

STEINBERG. But you're a businessman, like myself, Mr. Rick. Weren't you in on a percentage of the find?

RICK. Ten percent. The way he figured it would be worth over a hundred thousand. But he didn't figure on turning up dead.

STEINBERG. That's a lot of money – obviously someone else was figuring along the same lines. *(Steinberg notices* **SYDNEY***)* It's a very fascinating exhibit, Mr. Rick. If you'll excuse me.

*(***STEINBERG*** intercepts* **CAIRO***.)*

STEINBERG. When did she show up and what's she doing here?

*(***STEINBERG*** motions across the room to* **SYDNEY***.)*

CAIRO. She was here before you. Didn't you notice her? Mr. Rick hired her on as a singer. That is what she is.

STEINBERG. I know what she is, alright. Why didn't you tell me she was here?

CAIRO. The passport, Mr. Steinberg!

STEINBERG. Cairo, I can squash you like the little cockroach you are without so much as lifting my finger.

CAIRO. Then get me out of here! I'm tired of Mustique. Everywhere I go, the police are watching. Everything I do, every call I make, every sucker I take.

STEINBERG. Why should I help you, a two-bit police informer?

CAIRO. I haven't informed on you yet, Steinberg. How would you like to know where those photos are?

(STEINBERG grabs CAIRO by the lapels.)

CAIRO. *(cont.)* Not that I have them, but I think I know who does. I'll make you a deal. Two photos for one passport.

STEINBERG. *(releasing Cairo)* If you had them, Cairo, you'd be forcing them on me. And I'd kill you, just for the fun of it. To see the look of shock on your face.

CAIRO. That's what everyone likes about you, Mr. Steinberg. Your patience and business psychology.

(STEINBERG laughs and walks away. CAIRO begins to leave and is stopped by JEAN.)

JEAN. Mr. Cairo, about our little cruise?

CAIRO. Do you still want to go?

JEAN. I want what you have.

CAIRO. Hemorrhoids?

JEAN. The report. The one about the ERR submarine.

CAIRO. I don't have it. But I might be able to locate the photos –

JEAN. The photos are one thing. But it's the report I want most. I can make it very worth your while. I lost my passport once before. They're used to me.

CAIRO. I'll see what I can do, but I really don't know where it is. It isn't still hanging up?

JEAN. Think, Mr. Cairo. If it were, why would I be bribing you to find it?

CAIRO. Good point.

JEAN. Thank you, Mr. Cairo. I think we'll get along together just fine.

(CAIRO smiles and leaves. JEAN stops SYDNEY.)

JEAN. Pardon me, but haven't we met before?

SYDNEY. I don't think so? If you'll excuse me?

JEAN. About 15 minutes ago, I seem to remember seeing you come around from the shadows shortly after all the gunshots. I was just back there on the dock – well, looking at the view. It's quite a lovely view, isn't it?

SYDNEY. Exceptional, if you like creaky docks and locked up warehouses. Funny how I don't remember seeing you.

JEAN. Oh, I was there, alright. You seemed to be in quite a rush.

SYDNEY. The sound of gunfire frightens me.

JEAN. Really? Oh, well, you cover it well. No, you didn't look frightened in the least, quite controlled, as a matter of fact. Although now that I think of it, the gunfire had stopped by the time you appeared. You were so quiet, I almost didn't even notice you.

SYDNEY. Are you accusing me of something, Ms…?

JEAN. Jean Dijon. But of course not. What could you be guilty of? I'm just interested in how you learned to sneak around so quickly and quietly.

SYDNEY. I went to an all girl's school.

JEAN. That explains it. Tell me, do you remember those photos you noticed that were missing?

SYDNEY. One of them.

JEAN. Then how did you know two were missing?

SYDNEY. What are you getting at?

JEAN. Oh, nothing, really. It's just, you see, I'm a historian, and those particular photos would have fit nicely into something I'm presently working on.

SYDNEY. Are you accusing me of taking them?

JEAN. Certainly not, I just thought you might know of some way for me to get ahold of what seems to be missing from the exhibit. The money would be quite good. Have a nice evening, Miss…?

SYDNEY. Sydney.

JEAN. Sydney. How very American.

(RICK *has seen the conversation and starts towards* SYDNEY, *when he is intercepted by* SAM, *a bit tipsy.*)

SAM. Mr. Rick, sorry to take a shot at you like that this evening. But I'm from New York, remember? When people get bored in that town they decide to take pot-shots at cops – and we take pot shots back.

RICK. No damage done, Detective.

(**RICK** *motions a signal to* **CAIRO**, *who goes to the bar and gets a special drink.*)

SAM. You know, I didn't want to come down here. I don't particularly care for islands that don't have tunnels and bridges connecting them to a mainland. Some day a real big wave will come along and wash it so far out to sea no one'll see it again.

(**SAM** *finishes his drink.* **CAIRO** *hands Rick the new drink.*)

RICK. Maybe.

(**RICK** *hands* **SAM** *the drink, who nods thanks and drinks it.*)

SAM. That's strong stuff, what is it?

RICK. Club soda, alka seltzer, fresh coffee beans and a twist of lime.

SAM. That lime can do it to you every time. You ever been divorced? *(without waiting for an answer)* I just got divorced.

RICK. How long ago?

SAM. Six years.

RICK. That recent?

SAM. My wife didn't like being married to a cop. Every time I didn't come home she thought I was dead. She said she was tired of being a widow 52 times a year. It's rough on the spouse of a cop.

RICK. It's rough on the kids of a cop.

SAM. Your father was a cop?

RICK. My mother. She worked undercover in San Francisco, until she was killed by a trollycar she didn't see while tailing a suspect. I was thirteen, my sister was sixteen. My father didn't know what to do with us, so he dumped us on our aunt and became a traveling salesman. We saw him maybe once every two months.

SAM. I see my daughter once a week. We go to the movies. I buy her popcorn. She eats it. We both watch the movie. Thrilling, isn't it?

(During the last few lines, **CAIRO** *motions to* **RICK**, *who goes off to talk with him.* **SAM** *doesn't notice he's alone.* **SYDNEY** *joins him.)*

SYDNEY. How old is she?

SAM. Seven… I think. What does a New York City cop have in common with a seven-year-old girl who lives in Connecticut?

SYDNEY. You're her father.

SAM. Is that enough?

SYDNEY. It was for me. My parents split when I was seven. I lived with my mother in Santa Barbara. Once a week I went up to L.A. to see my dad.

SAM. Do you like your dad?

SYDNEY. I love him. He's my dad.

SAM. Thanks. Who are you anyway? A suspect or a friendly traveler passing through?

SYDNEY. Probably both. My name's Sydney. My folks wanted a boy. It didn't make any difference to me at the time. It still doesn't. You're finished here, aren't you?

SAM. In more ways than one. How could I have let her play me for the sap like that?

SYDNEY. You were lonely. She was pretty. It wasn't your fault.

SAM. It was, but thanks all the same. You're one hell of a gal, Sydney.

SYDNEY. Maybe, but thanks all the same. What's your first name?

SAM. Sam.

SYDNEY. Sam. That was my husband's name, but I still like it.

SAM. What happened?

SYDNEY. He got in with the wrong type of businessmen, the kind that have contracts made of cold steel, and are signed in blood. He became aggressive, moving up the ladder faster than some people would prefer. He became powerful and cold. He made enemies of people it's not safe to make enemies of. I wanted him to stop. He wanted me to leave.

SAM. So you came here?

SYDNEY. Island hopping. I loved that man more than anything. I still do. They bent him, changed him, eventually killed him. What do you do when someone kills the only thing in the whole world you really love?

SAM. Cry. Or get even.

SYDNEY. One's easier than the other. But I was going to be your shoulder for the evening, wasn't I, Sam?

SAM. Consider us even. Buy you a drink?

SYDNEY. No, how about just a place to sit in the darkness, alone next to a friendly face and a warm shoulder to rest on?

(They start to walk off together, when **SHEILA** *enters with a small suitcase. She looks at the displays.)*

SHEILA. RICK? CAIRO?

SAM/SYDNEY/STEINBERG/JEAN. *(shocked at her resemblance to* **MAUREEN** *)(to audience members)* But – I was sure she was dead!

(Black out. Second course is served.)

(Shaken, **SAM** *goes to the bar to get another drink. He goes from table to table asking people if* **SHEILA** *isn't* **MAUREEN**, *whom everyone just witnessed die. It is obvious how much he hated* **MAUREEN** *and is glad she's dead, because extraditing her looked like it would take a long time.)*

*(***CAIRO** *asks people if they know what became of the report. Hopefully someone will remember* **BEN** *took it. He'll show people the photos and offer to sell them for a passport. He points out that Adolf Hitler is in the one photo and reveals the rumor that Hitler visited Mustique in 1945, to arrange an escape route to Argentina.)*

*(***RICK** *shows* **SHEILA** *around, introducing her as the co-manager of the Cafe Noir and asking how their evening has been so far. She keeps trying to take her suitcase into the back, but* **RICK** *keeps stopping her.)*

(*JEAN moves from table to table asking about the report, the photos, and soliciting investors in her ERR recovery company looking for sunken treasure.*)

SCENE III

(Music intro. Lights up. **STEINBERG** *approaches* **SHEILA**, *who is frozen in fear.)*

STEINBERG. *(Clapping)* You're an incredible woman! How can they arrest someone who just died – in front of a room full of witnesses, no less? Your cunning is only exceeded by your allure.

(He kisses her hand. **SAM** *approaches her, drunk.* **STEINBERG** *steps away quickly.)*

SAM. *(tipsy)* What's this? Another of your nine lives? The staggering, the blood – Tell me, Laura, how'd you make it so convincing?

SHEILA. I don't know what you're talking about. And my name is Sheila, Sheila Wonderly.

SAM. God, not this again?

*(**SYDNEY** steers **SAM** away from **SHEILA**.)*

SYDNEY. Please – you'll have to excuse him, he's a bit drunk. You just look so familiar.

SHEILA. Well, I haven't the foggiest idea who you or your friends are. I just got back from a rather turbulent seaplane flight so if you don't mind – ?

*(**SHEILA** walks around **SYDNEY**, and almost into **JEAN**.)*

JEAN. I wouldn't believe it if I hadn't seen it all with my own eyes. I swore I saw those bullets hit you. But how could you have planned it out so well?

SHEILA. Is everyone around here crazy?

*(**SHEILA** starts towards the back room, when **CAIRO** enters from it and stops her.)*

CAIRO. Ms. Wonderly? So glad to see you back earlier than expected. But I really don't think you want to go into the back room just now?

SHEILA. Cairo, get out of my way. I'm going to the back room.

CAIRO. Mr. Rick has requested I detain you while he attends a matter that he'd rather you were shielded from.

SHEILA. Great, out here everyone's crazy and back there Rick's messing around with a sweet looking dame – is that it?

CAIRO. Well, you're not far off. But –

(She storms past CAIRO.)

CAIRO. I really don't think you want to –

(SHEILA screams a terrifying scream from the back room. She comes running out. RICK follows her closely.)

RICK. Cairo! I told you to stall her while I moved the –

SHEILA. That's me back there! I'm dead in the back office.

RICK. No, you're alive in the dining room. But there's a corpse that looks surprisingly like you in the back room, the sight of which nearly killed you. You know, until you walked in a few minutes ago, I never realized how much she looked like you.

SHEILA. I need a drink.

(CAIRO hands her a drink. She throws the drink in her face.)

CAIRO. Would you care for another? Maybe one to drink?

(She nods "yes" and hands the drink back to CAIRO, who exits to the bar. RICK wipes her face with his hanky.)

RICK. Sheila, I'm really glad you're back. How's your mother?

SHEILA. Fine, now that she's left my father. Maybe she'll kick her drinking problem next. Rick, what the hell's been going on here?

RICK. It's a long story. While you were gone, Cairo came up with the idea of hiring a singer and I came up with the idea of doing this exhibit, to attract more business.

SHEILA. It seems to be attracting the wrong kind of business.

RICK. *(motioning to a table)* Maybe you're right, but you shouldn't insult the customers in front of them.

SHEILA. I mean the corpse who looks like me in the back room and him *(motioning to* **STEINBERG***)*. Do you have any idea who he is?

RICK. Edward G. Steinberg, some acquaintance of Cairo's.

SHEILA. And that didn't tip you off? You're slipping, Rick. Steinberg is a big-time mobster wanted in several states for racketeering and murder.

RICK. Who, him?

SHEILA. Yes him, and don't point. He financed my father's bid for the governorship a few years ago.

RICK. Wait. Your father is a big-time holy roller, isn't he?

SHEILA. So he was a natural front for some gangsters to pick as a candidate for Governor. Politicians and evangelist preachers will both do and say anything for money. Election day fell on my sixteenth birthday. My father spent the day at his campaign headquarters and my mother spent it at a rehab clinic. Steinberg was a real dapper dan back then, snappy dresser, charismatic – he was the only one to come to wish me happy birthday. The next day the FBI was after Steinberg for ballot stuffing. My father confessed to the feds. To get even, Steinberg sent my father photos he had secretly taken on my birthday, when he seduced me. Now he doesn't even remember me. But I never forgot him, and God knows I've tried.

RICK. Sort of a double-barreled welcome home, I guess.

SHEILA. Now what about my dead twin?

CAIRO. *(returning with drink)* Some hit-woman our drunken American cop came to take back to the states. But someone iced her on the docks out back, along with her lawyer brother. There were so many bullets flying out there in the dark, it was almost like the fourth of July in my old neighborhood. Actually, it was like that the fourth of every month in my old neighborhood, along with the fifth and the sixth and the –

RICK. *(escorting her out)* Come on out front for some fresh air and I'll fill you in. You should know what to expect before Inspector Rigfield gets here.

SHEILA. *(exiting)* Rigfield made full inspector?

*(***CAIRO*** *pulls the photos out of his jacket.)*

CAIRO. Adolph, you disappoint me.

JEAN. Well, Mr. Cairo, it seems you are a very fast worker.

(She steps out from the shadows and takes the photos, examining them.)

JEAN. Do you have the report, as well?

*(***CAIRO*** *smiles and hands it to her.* ***JEAN*** *gets ready to kiss* ***CAIRO*** *when* ***STEINBERG*** *steps out of the shadows.)*

STEINBERG. Well, well, well, Cairo. Selling to a competitor? That's not very loyal of you. Nor is it very safe.

*(***STEINBERG*** *pulls out a gun.)*

STEINBERG. I'll take those, sweetheart.

*(***JEAN*** *looks at them, reluctant to give them up.)*

STEINBERG. Don't be a fool. There are things that are simply not worth dying for.

*(***CAIRO*** *takes the photos and report from* ***JEAN*** *and hands them to* ***STEINBERG****, who starts to put his gun away.)*

STEINBERG. Thank you, Cairo. Now...

*(***JEAN*** *pulls out a gun.)*

JEAN. Now, you can return those items to me, Mr. Steinberg.

*(***CAIRO*** *takes them from* ***STEINBERG*** *and hands them to* ***JEAN****.)*

JEAN. Thank you, Mr. Cairo. Mr. Steinberg, may I advise you to hand your gun to Mr Cairo. As you said yourself, some things are simply not worth dying for.

*(***STEINBERG*** *hands* ***CAIRO*** *the gun.)*

JEAN. Now all that's left is for us to find that chart Mr. Temple had. Mr. Steinberg, you wouldn't happen to know where that might be?

STEINBERG. I wouldn't tell you if I did. And you won't shoot me either.

JEAN. *(putting her gun away)* Quite right, Mr. Steinberg. But someone tonight has gotten a little trigger happy. We certainly don't want to become the next bit of target practice. Now the true challenge, Mr. Cairo. Can you find what's left?

STEINBERG. If you do and give it to her, you'll be spending eternity as a decoration on the coral reefs.

CAIRO. I really don't know anything about a chart or where it might be.

JEAN. That's what you said about the report. The night is young, Mr. Cairo. *(She takes out her key and hands it to him)* I'm over at the Blue Parrot, room 1948. Do come over when you find the chart. I'll just finish my drink and then go over and get comfortable. Good night, Mr. Steinberg.

(She exits to the bar to finish her drink. STEINBERG *snaps his fingers, and* CAIRO *reluctantly hands him back his gun.)*

CAIRO. Save your breath, Steinberg, I know what you're going to say before you say it. Just remember, I offered it to you first.

STEINBERG. Cairo…

CAIRO. Can it, Steinberg. If you want to shoot, go right ahead. But try to make it in the center of the back. I just bought the suit.

(CAIRO turns and walks away from STEINBERG without looking back. STEINBERG *raises his gun and fires it in the air.* CAIRO *drops.* RICK *and* SHEILA *come rushing back in. They help* CAIRO *up, who checks himself for bullet holes.* STEINBERG *laughs.* SHEILA *walks up to* STEINBERG *and slaps him. He lowers the gun to between her eyes. She doesn't flinch.* SAM, CAIRO, *and* RICK *all take a step towards* STEINBERG, *cautiously.)*

STEINBERG. No one slaps around Edward G. Steinberg.

(SHEILA slaps him again.)

SHEILA. The first one was for Cairo. The second for me.

STEINBERG You really have a death wish, don't you little lady?

SHEILA. You already killed me once, Steinberg.

(STEINBERG looks around nervously.)

SHEILA. When I was sixteen. When my name was Sheilda Schickelmeyer.

STEINBERG/JEAN/CAIRO. Schickelmeyer?

SHEILA. Now you see why I changed it. But my father had his own professional name, Billy Ritz.

STEINBERG. *(lowering gun)* You couldn't be Reverend Billy Ritz's sexy little daughter? Well, well, well!

(SHEILA slaps him again.)

STEINBERG. Stop that. After all this time, you can't hate me that much.

(She gets ready to slap him again. He grabs her hand, then puts the gun in it.)

STEINBERG. Here. Let me make your day.

(She raises the gun and points it between his eyes.)

STEINBERG. Go ahead, pull the trigger. Not too hard or the gun will jerk and you could miss, even at this close range. I'd end up with only a flesh wound. Squeeze the trigger. Straight and steady. Squeeze it the same way you squeeze –

(She cocks the gun. There is an awkward pause. RICK and SAM move closer to her.)

RICK. It's up to you, but neither Cairo nor I are cleaning up the mess.

SAM. Just put the gun down. Even if you could do it, this is a room full of witnesses.

STEINBERG. But this is the Cafe Noir – where no one ever witnesses anything. Go on. You've been wanting to do this for so long, you're not really going to let it slip through your fingers are you? Go on, I dare you!

(She thinks for a moment, then lowers her aim to his crotch. **STEINBERG** *covers his crotch as* **RICK** *rushes* **SHEILA,** *moving her aim off to the side just as she fires the gun. He takes the gun.)*

STEINBERG. *(cont.)* Judas priest!

SHEILA. We still have a score to settle, Steinberg.

(She turns and walks away.)

STEINBERG. Obviously we don't share the same taste in music. My gun, Mr. Rick?

RICK. I think it would be safer if I left it behind the bar. You can collect it when you leave.

(He puts it behind the bar. **STEINBERG** *laughs.)*

STEINBERG. I don't care where you put it, though I have a few suggestions, Mr. Rick. But I won't have to collect it when I leave, because this place is soon to be mine.

*(***STEINBERG** *holds up a mortgage contract.)*

I assumed your mortgage from the St. Vincent Trust Company. It seems they didn't trust you much. Unless you can make good on all your outstanding mortgage payments by midnight tonight, I'm foreclosing tomorrow.

RICK. *(to audience member)* You think you can spot me a couple of bucks? Not much, something around ten thousand?

*(***SYDNEY** *pulls a grey envelope out of her purse and hands it to* **RICK.** *)*

SYDNEY. You might say it's my mad money. I'm not even sure how much is in there.

RICK. I can't.

(He hands it back. She thrusts it on **SHEILA.** *)*

SYDNEY. Please, take it.

SAM. What would a gangster on the lam want with a Caribbean cafe?

STEINBERG. I'm a businessman, detective, and this place

seems to do a fair amount of business.

SAM. And as you are wanted in several states, you need a new place to set up operations.

STEINBERG. Nonsense, Copper. We're just on vacation. *(to male audience member)* Ain't that right?

SAM. *(to same man)* Wilber "the weasel" Weinstock – wanted in three states for counterfeiting, forgery, falsifying legal documents, and *(gesturing to his date)* corrupting the morals of a minor. I thought you were spending five to ten in Levenworth?

STEINBERG. He broke out with the assistance of *(gesturing to another audience member)* Louie here.

SAM. *(to 2nd man)* Louie "the Loone" Labrano. Multiple convictions for aiding and abetting, assault, larceny, resisting arrest, and indecent exposure. It'll be five to ten before they let you back in a Woolworths. So the gang's all here?

STEINBERG. Of course. *(to a female audience member)* Isn't that right, Petunia?

SAM. Petunia "Peaches" Peretti – Fraud, extortion, prostitution, white slavery, and failure to yield right of way. She's got more moving violations than the entire state of New Jersey.

STEINBERG. We've found ourselves a new home, far from your reach, Copper.

SHEILA. Don't try moving in too fast. *(to **RICK**)* There's exactly ten thousand here, Rick. Maybe if we took it just as a loan –

STEINBERG. Of course I'd have to collect penalties and interest, at 20%. That would mean an additional two thousand.

RICK. Well, maybe with the bar tab after tonight – especially the way this table's drinking – *(motioning to bartender)* Coffee all around.

STEINBERG. I sort of like you, Mr. Just Plain Rick. So I'll give you a sporting chance. But I have to warn you, I'm a rather lucky man when it comes to cards.

(**STEINBERG** *pulls out a deck and begins shuffling.*
RICK *nods to* **CAIRO**, *who pulls out gambling chips.*)

RICK. What's your pleasure, Steinberg. Blackjack, poker?

STEINBERG. Come on, Mr. Rick. This is the island of
Mustique. We should play something much more
befitting the international atmosphere. Baccarat. Our
French representative shall deal, and our police officer can hold the bets.

(**STEINBERG** *hands the deck to* **JEAN**, *then pulls out
some thousand dollar bills and hands them to* **SAM**.)

STEINBERG. A Madison a chip. There's ten thousand there,
to match yours. Mr. Cairo?

(**CAIRO** *counts out ten chips for* **STEINBERG**.)

(*Everyone freezes.* **RICK** *turns to the audience.*)

RICK. Okay folks, here we are again. I'm not sure how
much we have stashed in the safe or how much we'll
bring in tonight at the bar. Maybe it's two Madison,
maybe not. What I do know is that I don't know how to
play Baccarat. Maybe I'll be lucky and can win against
Steinberg and maybe not. How many say play it safe
and deal myself out?

(*audience vote*)

And how many say lay my cards on the table and play
his game?

(*audience vote*)

VERSION A: If they vote for him to play:

(**SHEILA** *hands her envelope to* **SAM**. **CAIRO** *counts out ten chips to her. She hands them to* **RICK**.)

VERSION B: If the audience votes for him not to play:

RICK. No thank you, Mr. Steinberg. I'll take my chances on the thirstiness of the crowd tonight.

(**SHEILA** *hands the money to* **SAM**.)

SHEILA. Deal me in.

RICK. What?

SHEILA. I'm the co-owner aren't I? Well I'd rather not be a co-owner of nothing without a fight.

(**CAIRO** *hands her ten chips. [The rest of the scene progresses the same, but with* **SHEILA** *playing* **RICK***'s part.]*)

BOTH VERSIONS CONTINUE:

SYDNEY. *(stage whisper to* **RICK***)* A word of warning. Steinberg's a master at sleight of hand. He never –

STEINBERG. In case you've forgotten, the game's a sort of French blackjack. To win you have to have a point total whose last digit is closest to nine. Shall we begin?

(**JEAN** *deals one card down and one card up to both of them. – The deck must be pre-stacked, using only black cards. First deal:* **STEINBERG** *face down, two.* **RICK** *[***SHEILA***] face down, Jack.* **STEINBERG** *face up, five.* **RICK** *[***SHEILA***] face up, eight. –* **STEINBERG** *puts in a chip, as does* **RICK** *[***SHEILA***].* **STEINBERG** *looks at his down card, then rubs it between his hands.*)

JEAN. *(to* **STEINBERG***)* Mr. Steinberg, you are showing a five. Card? No card?

(**STEINBERG** *nods.*)

JEAN. Card *(she deals him a two)* A two, total showing seven. *(to* **RICK***[***SHEILA***])* Mr. Just Plain Rick (Ms. Wonderly), you are showing eight. Card? No card?

*(**RICK** [**SHEILA**] taps on the table.)*

JEAN. No card. All bets please.

STEINBERG. You're looking good, Mr. Rick (Ms. Wonderly). How about two thou on the first hand?

*(**STEINBERG** puts in two chips.)*

RICK (SHEILA). Here's looking at you, Kid.

*(He (she) puts in two chips. **RICK** (**SHEILA**) turns his (her) card over.)*

JEAN. Eighteen for Mr. Just Plain Rick (Ms. Wonderly).

*(**STEINBERG** turns his card over.)*

JEAN. Nine for Mr. Steinberg. Game, Mr. Steinberg.

STEINBERG. Shall we up the stakes, Mr. Rick (Ms. Wonderly)?

RICK (SHEILA). How do you mean?

STEINBERG. *(dropping it on table)* With the mortgage for your cafe.

RICK (SHEILA). Against what, Steinberg? I only have seven thousand left.

STEINBERG. That – and Cafe Noir's Ms. Wonderly, herself.

RICK. I (You) can't ask her to do that. It sounds like the premise to a few movies –

STEINBERG. Best two out of three hands?

SHEILA. I'm game. Deal.

SAM. But –

SHEILA. I said deal.

(There is an awkward pause.)

STEINBERG. You heard the lady.

RICK. I'd like to hear from our newly hired lady. Sydney, how about a song?

(Everyone looks at him like he's crazy.)

EVERYONE. Now?

RICK. To calm the nerves. *(If VERSION B, **RICK** will now take over playing the game from **SHEILA**)* That song they always play on the radio – "You're aces with me."

(Music begins as **SYDNEY** *sings.)*

SYDNEY.

I'VE NEVER BEEN A FOOL
I'VE ALWAYS PLAYED IT COOL
SCHOOLED IN THE GAMES OF CHANCE
I NEVER TRUSTED ROMANCE

MAYBE YOU STACKED THE CARDS
BABY, I FELL
BUT HARD
STILL I LOSE GRACEFULLY
HONEY, YOU'RE ACES WITH ME

*(***STEINBERG*** is impatient as* **JEAN** *deals very slowly, listening to the song. –* **STEINBERG** *card down, King.* **RICK** *card down, six.* **STEINBERG** *card up, eight.* **RICK** *card up, ten. – She must be done dealing by the time* **SYDNEY** *sings "You're aces with me."* **RICK** *signals* **SYDNEY***, who moves behind* **STEINBERG** *to play with his hair and look at his card. Since* **STEINBERG** *is supposed to be cheating, her first lyric "clues" won't match the card he's dealt).*

SYDNEY.

YOU DEALT A HAND I KNEW
YOU MUST HAVE FELT IT, TOO

(She holds up two fingers. She continues to hum the song during the following dialogue, dropping in lyrics at the appropriate moments.)

JEAN. *(to Steinberg)* Eight up, Mr. Steinberg. Card, no card?

*(***STEINBERG*** nods, is dealt an ace.)*

JEAN. Ace, makes nine showing. Mr. Just Plain Rick, ten showing. Card, no card?

*(***RICK*** motions for more time and looks at* **SYDNEY***, who looks at* **STEINBERG***'s card again and is surprised to see he has a king.)*

SYDNEY.

YOU TREATED ME LIKE A – KING?

(**STEINBERG** *looks up at her, puzzled. She goes back to humming as* **RICK** *motions for another card.* **JEAN** *deals him a three.*)

JEAN. Three, makes thirteen showing. Cards please.

(*Both men flip over their cards.*)

JEAN. Nineteen, Mr. Rick, Nineteen Mr. Steinberg. Tie, new deal.

(*There is a music interlude as* **JEAN** *collects the cards and deals again –* **STEINBERG** *down, five.* **RICK** *down, seven.* **STEINBERG** *up, four.* **RICK** *up, five. –* **SYDNEY** *moves behind* **STEINBERG** *and looks at his newly dealt card.*)

SYDNEY.

YOU PLAY THE GAME SO WELL
BUT I KNOW THE SCORE
YOU MUST BELIEVE
I HAVE BEEN THERE BEFORE

(*She holds up four fingers.* **STEINBERG** *starts to turn around, and she runs her fingers through his hair as she continues to hum.*)

JEAN. Four showing, Mr. Steinberg. Card, no card?

(*He waves his hand.*)

JEAN.

No card. Five showing, Mr. Rick. Card, no card?

(**STEINBERG** *plays with his card [supposedly switching it] as* **RICK** *nods.* **JEAN** *deals him a six.* **RICK** *flips over his cards.*)

JEAN. Six makes eleven showing, Mr. Rick totals eighteen. Mr. Steinberg?

(*He shows his card to be a five.*)

JEAN. A five for nine. Game, Steinberg. New deal.
RICK. Five?

(He glares at **SYDNEY**, *who looks apologetic.* **JEAN** *collects the cards and deals during the music interlude. –* **STEINBERG** *down, nine of spades.* **RICK** *down, ten.* **STEINBERG** *up, King.* **RICK** *up, Jack.)*

SYDNEY.

SOMEHOW YOU'VE CHANGED THE RULES
I WAS A TEN -DER FOOL
I NEVER MEANT TO BE
HONEY YOU'RE ACES WITH ME

(She hums under the dialogue.)

JEAN. Mr. Steinberg, ten showing. Card, no card?

(He waves his hand and palms the card.)

JEAN. No card. Mr. Rick, ten showing. Card, no card?

(He looks at **SYDNEY**, *who looks at* **STEINBERG**'s *card.)*

SYDNEY. *(shocked)*

DRESSED TO THE NINES!

(Music pauses as everyone stares at her. **RICK** *nods, music resumes, and* **JEAN** *deals him the nine of spades.* **RICK** *turns his card over.)*

JEAN. Nine of spades, making twenty nine for Mr. Rick. Mr. Steinberg?

*(***SYDNEY** *sits on* **STEINBERG**'s *lap, stopping him as he attempts to plam the card again.)*

SYDNEY.

YOU'RE ACES WITH ME.

*(***STEINBERG** *pushes her off his lap to the floor and throws the card down.)*

JEAN. Nine of spades, making nineteen. Tie, new deal.

SHEILA. Two nine of spades?

STEINBERG. Oops.

*(***SHEILA** *and* **RICK** *grab the mortgage.* **STEIMBERG** *pulls another gun.)*

RICK. Never go anywhere without a spare, eh, Steinberg?

STEINBERG. *(taking mortgage)* That's right, smart guy. Do you seriously think I'd ever sign this document over to you? Not on my life. Keep the twenty thou. There's more than that just waiting beneath the darkened sea. Your gun, Miss Dijon. And the report, of course.

(She hands them to him.)

STEINBERG. Mr. Cairo – it's time you do some nocturnal diving for me. *(to* **RICK***)* We'll take the boat you prepared for the deceased, as we'll be needing the equipment you've so thoughtfully supplied.

SAM. You can't take that boat. It's sealed off as a crime scene.

STEINBERG. You're one funny guy, Mr. Detective. *(waving gun at everyone)* Why don't we make it a family outing. All hands on deck, we're all going for a little diving party. Don't worry about your cafe, it'll be watched by the rest of my gang while we're gone. Now let's not delay – it's Bon Voyage time.

*(***STEINBERG*** waves his gun, forcing* **RICK, SAM, CAIRO, SHEILA, JEAN,** *and* **SYDNEY** *to exit.)*

SCENE IV

(Music intro. Blackout. There is the sound of a fog horn. The sound of a boat can be heard along with the sound of waves breaking against the ships bow. The foghorn sounds again. There is the sound of a splash. Voices shout in the dark.)

SAM. What was that?

JEAN. Someone fell overboard!

SHEILA. Who?

CAIRO. It's too dark and foggy.

RICK. Someone grab the lifesaver!

SYDNEY. Where is the lifesaver?

CAIRO. I've got it?

JEAN. Let go of me.

CAIRO. Oh, sorry.

RICK. You know, I don't think this boat has a lifesaver.

SHEILA. Yes it does. I saw it.

JEAN. Where?

SHEILA/CAIRO/SAM/SYDNEY/RICK. Over there!

SAM. Wait. I found it. But where do I throw it?

RICK/SHEILA/CAIRO/SYDNEY/JEAN. Over here!

SAM. I can't see a damned thing. Well, here it goes.

SHEILA. OUCH. Watch where you're throwing that thing, fellah.

SAM. Sorry.

EVERYONE. Give it to me, I'll throw it... No, I'll throw it... Where is it?

*(The foghorn sounds again. The boat sounds fade out. Lights up. All the characters, except **STEINBERG**, have reentered. Each holds a drink.)*

SAM. I can't believe this.

JEAN. They do say bad things happen in threes.

SHEILA. Well, it couldn't have happened to a better third than Steinberg.

CAIRO. Right over the back of the boat *(snaps fingers)* just like that!

SYDNEY. Well, it certainly was rough out there with those waves and the fog.

SAM. It was his own fault for demanding to stand at the back of the boat like that and barking orders at us.

JEAN. He was so busy guarding that chart he found beneath Ben Temple's body that he must have lost his footing in the darkness, with all that water splashing around the deck.

SHEILA. Top of the world one moment –

CAIRO. Bottom of the sea the next.

SYDNEY. And no one around to even see him fall over.

(They all raise their glasses as a toast and drink.)

RICK. Unless he didn't fall at all.

(They all spit their drink back into their glasses. **RIGFIELD** *enters.)*

RIGFIELD. Mr. Steinberg fell, alright –

(They all smile and sip their drinks.)

RIGFIELD. When a .32 calibre slug knocked him off balance, that is.

(They all spit their drinks back into their glasses again.)

SHEILA. Deputy Inspector Rigfield, so nice to see you again.

RIGFIELD. That's full inspector now, Ms. Wonderly.

RICK. Congratulations, Rigfield. How'd you do it?

RIGFIELD. By not going easy on the likes of your clientele, Mr. Archer. We retrieved Mr. Steinberg's body after it got itself stuck to the underside of one of those clear bottom sightseeing boats. American gangster is the not the typical fish you might except to see around these waters – although I'm sure it's quite common around your watering holes, eh, Detective Lyric?

SAM. They usually weight them down pretty good so they don't come up for air for several years.

RIGFIELD. Yes, of course, the famous New York cement overshoes. You realize that by taking that ship out you not only tampered with the scene of the crime but moved a corpse?

SAM. Mr. Steinberg did have us all at gunpoint, Inspector. A snub nose .38 Smith & Westin better known as a Saturday Night Special.

RIGFIELD. I bloody well know what a Saturday Night Special is, Detective. No sign of that kind of hardware on the deceased, however.

SAM. Then it's still on the aft deck of the boat or it dropped overboard when he did. I believe you'll still find the body of Ben Temple at the bow.

RIGFIELD. *(annoyed at* **SAM***'s know-it-all manner)* Right. And I bloody well expect I'll find that other corpse, *(checking notes)* Maureen Temple, in the place corpses seem to desire frequenting the most, the back room of the Cafe Noir?

RICK. We certainly wouldn't want to disappoint you, Inspector.

RIGFIELD. It's never a disappointment coming to the Cafe Noir, just a damn nuisance. I'll just have a quick look at the corpses and then be back to begin taking statements. *(To* **SAM***, facetious)* I'm sure, Detective, that you won't allow anyone to leave.

SAM. My pleasure to be of assistance, Inspector.

RIGFIELD. *(annoyed)* Right.

*(***RIGFIELD*** exits to the back room.)*

JEAN. *(to* **SHEILA***)* Shickelmeyer?

SHEILA. Yes, why?

JEAN. Such a coincidence, is it not?

SHEILA. How so?

JEAN. Just with the rumors – and the photograph Mr. Archer found for the display.

SHEILA. I'm sorry, but I still don't follow you.

(**JEAN** *hands her the photo of Hitler on a submarine.*)

JEAN. Proof that Adolf Schickelgruber, or some say Schickelmeyer, did visit Mustique in 1945. Of course, he was better known by his professional name – Adolf Hitler.

RICK. *(taking photo)* Thank you for returning part of my exhibit. It cost me a pretty penny, too. Cairo, you seem to know everything seedy there is to know around here –

CAIRO. *(aside to audience)* Is that a compliment?

RICK. What's this rumor all about?

CAIRO. Mustique was believed to be part of Hitler's escape route to Argentina. Supposedly his submarine struck a coral reef and sunk here.

SAM. Wait a second. You expect us to believe that Hitler escaped Germany and then his submarine rammed a reef off Mustique Island? And I thought I was drinking heavily.

JEAN. Of course it's just a foolish rumor. Nothing to take seriously.

CAIRO. Really? Then what about the photo and that report of an SOS from a German ERR submarine sinking on a nearby reef? The report you and Steinberg were ready to kill over?

SHEILA. An ERR submarine? Err? What's that, an angry U-boat?

SYDNEY. Der Einsatzstab Reichsleiter Rosenberg. The organization the Nazis set up to loot Europe of their art treasures. It was based at the Jeu de Paume Gallery in Paris during the occupation and directed the distribution and hiding of millions of masterpieces. Researching the ERR was my late husband's obsession. He uncovered references that Hitler planned on sending a submarine loaded with statues, gold and other treasures to Argentina near the end of the war. Sort of a fascist retirement plan.

RICK. Did Steinberg and your husband know each other by any chance?

SYDNEY. Yes. I suppose it was my husband that started Steinberg on this crusade.

JEAN. One you have been following as well.

(**SYDNEY** *looks at* **JEAN.** **SAM** *looks at* **SYDNEY.**)

JEAN. Come now, don't expect us to believe you ended up here on Mustique by pure coincidence?

SYDNEY. Perhaps more like destiny. Interestingly enough, my husband's research also disclosed that there was a Vishy assistant curator at the Museum at the time who was a key figure in the plan. After the liberation of Paris, she was killed by an angry mob for collaboration with the enemy. Her name was Jean Dijon.

CAIRO. Jean Dijon?

JEAN. Oui. She was my grandmother.

(**RIGFIELD** *reenters.*)

RIGFIELD. Grandmother of mercy. That's Miss Wonderly dead back there!

SHEILA. I thought the same thing at first, myself.

RIGFIELD. I mean – Well, thank goodness it's not you.

SHEILA. Why, Inspector, I never knew you cared.

SAM. Have you looked over the boat yet, Inspector?

(**RIGFIELD** *turns to* **SAM,** *getting more annoyed at his directing of the investigation.*)

RIGFIELD. As a matter of fact, I went straight out and gave it a quick once-over before coming back to peek into that back room. Thank you for inquiring. Now –

JEAN. Did you happen to see a nautical chart?

RIGFIELD. No. I saw the bloody corpse of one Ben Temple near the bow and I saw virtually no blood around the aft of the boat, indicating that Mr. Steinberg's assailant shot him at point-blank range. Coroner says the bullet got lodged in the sternum, so it was the force of the shot that sent him right over the edge.

RICK. Point-blank range?

> **(RIGFIELD** *walks up to* **RICK** *and places his finger on* **RICK***'s chest.)*

RIGFIELD. According to the burn marks on his jacket, about this close. I'd consider that point-blank range, wouldn't you? Odd thing was, the deceased did have a Belgium made .22 Browning in his pocket.

JEAN. That was my gun, Inspector. Mr. Steinberg took it from me before we disembarked. Did the body have a chart on it, perhaps?

RIGFIELD. Three people are dead and the only blasted thing this lady is interested in is some balmy chart!

RICK. Because it might be a map to a sunken treasure, and it started out this evening in the hands of Ben Temple.

RIGFIELD. The bloody stiff on the bow of the boat?

SAM. Very good, Inspector. It seems that Temple, Steinberg, and Mademoiselle Dijon here were all racing after the same pot of gold – a sunken Nazi submarine.

RIGFIELD. *(Laughs)* Come on now, you're just ribbing my tickles. No one's fool enough to believe that old fable about Adolf Hitler sinking in a submarine off Mustique? The black market churns out these doctored photos of dear Adolph on a sub in Mustique bay, meanwhile, behind him are houses that weren't built until two years after the war. It's Mustique's version of the deed to the Brooklyn Bridge. I've never actually met anyone dim enough to buy one.

> **(RICK** *hands* **RIGFIELD** *the photo.* **RIGFIELD** *looks at it and laughs.)*

RIGFIELD. Until now, Mr. Rick.

RICK. You can rub it in later, Rigfield, but something like that rumor seems to figure prominently into these recent three homicides.

RIGFIELD. How's that?

CAIRO. It's an ERR submarine everyone's after, Inspector. Supposedly loaded with gold and masterpieces stolen by the Germans during the war.

RIGFIELD. Err? What's that supposed to be? An angry U-boat?

SHEILA. I tried that punch line already, Inspector. Then this woman, who was hired while I was gone as a singer in the cafe I'm half owner in – explained it all with a wonderful textbook answer. It seems she's known about this submerged catch all along. Though she's been very quiet about it.

RIGFIELD. Really? Well, she's a name you left off your suspect list, Detective Lyric. And we mustn't underestimate our dear Mr. Cairo?

CAIRO. Me? I was just a hired hand?

RIGFIELD. Hired to do what? Sergeant Instone tells me you've plea bargained to appear as a witness for the prosecution on a major smuggling case, but now you've got cold feet.

CAIRO. It's not cold feet, it's the survival instinct.

RIGFIELD. Call it whatever you like, but the fact remains you're desperate to get as far away from this island and the arms of the St. Vincent law as possible!

CAIRO. What? Me leave beautiful Mustique?

RIGFIELD. Come out with it, Cairo. You've probably spent every minute since you've been set free trying to buy someone's passport. *(To audience member)* Hasn't he?

(They'll answer "Yes." **CAIRO** *will growl at them.)*

CAIRO. Okay, sure I'm trying to escape this gray tropical island where everyone seems to be a cliche from some film noir movie. But that's hardly a motive for murder, Inspector.

SAM. Unless Steinberg was someone you were going to be forced to testify against. You knew if you did he'd have you bumped off. So killing him first would be sort of self-defense.

CAIRO. You're not going to let this out-of-towner tell you how to run your investigation, are you, Inspector Rigfield?

RIGFIELD. Certainly not. Did you, Mr. Cairo, have any business dealings with Mr. Steinberg previous to tonight?

CAIRO. Well – sure, on occasion.

RIGFIELD. And the evidence that you agreed to in your plea bargain – did any of that information relate to Mr. Steinberg?

CAIRO. Well –

RIGFIELD. I'll just get it straight from the prosecutor's office anyway, Cairo, so you might as well come clean with it.

CAIRO. Yes – but –

RIGFIELD. Thank you, Mr Cairo, for clarifying your motive. Now we come to Mr. Archer and Ms. Wonderly, who are so far behind on their mortgage payments that talk is the bank's putting the Cafe Noir on the block.

SAM. They already did, and Steinberg bought it.

(**RIGFIELD** *looks annoyed.*)

SHEILA. Are you trying to implicate us in this?

SAM. Trying? Steinberg was foreclosing, taking your Cafe Noir for himself. He bet Mr. Rick the mortgage and then cheated him out of $10,000 at cards. And you hated Steinberg for taking advantage of you when you were a not so sweet sixteen, so much so that you were ready to plug him right here in front of witnesses. Revenge is the strongest of motives on the police blotter.

SHEILA. Is that so? Then you have the strongest motive, mister incompetent detective.

RIGFIELD. *(Smiling)* Him? You dare say? Do tell.

CAIRO. Didn't Sgt. Instone tell you that our good visiting detective here followed the dying Maureen into the cafe with his gun drawn and several rounds missing?

(**RIGFIELD** *smiles at* **SAM** *and jots down a note.*)

SHEILA. And from what I hear, Maureen was the floozy he let roll him in the sack so she could plug a police informer our dear detective was supposed to be protecting. I'll bet that flushed a years' worth of New York's finest work down to the East River. It was in the papers.

(RIGFIELD looks at a newspaper on a table, then turns and smiles at SAM, who looks nervous.)

SAM. Okay, so Samuel Rocco was my responsibility, but –

CAIRO. Then he finds her here and it looks like an uphill fight to get her extricated. Thus adding insult to injury.

RICK. *(remembering something)* Earlier this evening I remember seeing Maureen talking with Steinberg.

CAIRO. But it sure looks like Steinberg hired Maureen to make that hit in New York.

SHEILA. If that's not a few strong revenge motives implicating Mr. Manhattan Detective in all three murders, then I'm a virgin.

SAM. This is ludicrous. I'm not going to defend myself against an ex-hooker and a convicted blackmarketeer.

RIGFIELD. You'll get a chance to defend yourself to a judge if you don't speak up, Detective. And in the future, you should refer to Ms. Wonderly's previous occupation as an escort. A very well-known one in these parts, but certainly never a hooker.

SHEILA. Why, thank you again, Inspector.

RIGFIELD. You're still a major suspect, Ms. Wonderly. Which I'm sure will annoy the police commissioner, as you were one of his favorite pastimes. Recently he's been seen in the company of her *(points to audience member)*.

SHEILA. *(to pointed out woman)* If you cut out some fur and glue it to the inside, after awhile you won't even notice you're wearing handcuffs.

SAM. Maybe Steinberg silenced Ben and Maureen before I could get her extradited?

RICK. What calibre was Steinberg shot with, Inspector?

RIGFIELD. A .32

RICK. And what is your guess as to the calibre that killed Maureen and Ben Temple?

SAM. A .32.

(**RIGFIELD** *looks annoyed at* **SAM.**)

RIGFIELD. Possibly a .32. Are you trying to make a case that all three were done in by the same killer?

RICK. I'm not sure. Just fishing.

RIGFIELD. Well, the bait's not very good. A .32 is an extremely common calibre around these parts. Small and accurate.

RICK. Does anyone remember seeing who stole the old reports from the exhibit earlier this evening?

(Hopefully someone in the audience will remember **BEN** *took them. If not,* **SYDNEY** *will.)*

SYDNEY. You know, now that I think about it, I do seem to remember seeing that lawyer Ben Temple take them. But didn't Mr. Cairo turn them over to you, Mademoiselle Dijon, for your passport later this evening?

CAIRO. Okay, so I got them off the dead body on the boat during the serving of one of the dinner courses. They weren't doing him any good at the time.

SHEILA. And they're not doing you any good right now, Cairo. Other than implicating you.

RICK. Lets face it, Rigfield. All of us had a motive of some kind to deep six Steinberg. The problem is –

RIGFIELD. The problem is putting up with your constant meddling and theorizing. I'm the inspector the government of St. Vincent saw fit to place in charge of investigations pertaining to the island of Mustique.

SAM. So that's who to blame.

RIGFIELD. *(to* **SAM***)* Oh, think you're bloody smart, eh, New York Shamus? Well, it wasn't me that allowed someone under my protection to get knocked off and then botched picking up the trigger. Maybe you offed Steinberg because you knew you won't be able to extradite him? Maybe Steinberg killed himself because he couldn't find Adolph Hitler's submarine? How about this? Maybe the submarine killed all of them because it didn't want to be found?

RICK. Maybe it would help to get some outside opinions, Rigfield? How about if we ask everyone here to write down their own deductions on whodunit and why? Who knows, maybe one of them will point us in the right direction?

SAM. That's the stupidest idea I've heard yet.

RIGFIELD. I think it's a grand idea. Alright, folks. If you would all be so kind as to jot down who you think is the killer or killers and why. Maybe you can help speed the serving of just desserts.

(Dessert is served. Characters mingle implicating each other while **RIGFIELD** *and* **RICK** *collect the sleuth sheets.)*

FINALE

(Music. Lights up. Everyone is present. All sleuth sheets have been collected.)

RICK. Folks, I would like to propose a toast. To Mr. Steinberg, a gangster, a card shark, and an all around nasty sort of guy. The world's not going to miss someone like Steinberg, but the law is the law, and his murderer must be brought to justice. Isn't that so, Inspector Rigfield?

RIGFIELD. That's the way it's always been and has to always be.

RICK. The first question is whether Steinberg killed Maureen and Ben Philips and if not, who did? Next, did the same person who fed Maureen some of her own medicine give a dosage to Steinberg as well, or did someone else beat them to the punch?

SAM. *(still drinking)* Who cares? They all deserved it. Live by the sword, burn by the matches.

RIGFIELD. Passing judgement isn't up to you or me, Detective. It's up to the courts alone.

RICK. Maybe there really is something to this missing submarine. And maybe there are people desparate enough to kill for it. But you, Inspector Rigfield, revealed the most important piece of the puzzle.

RIGFIELD. I did? – I mean, I did. *(to RICK)* What was that?

RICK. That he was killed at pointblank range.

(RICK walks up to SAM and places his finger in SAM's chest.)

RICK. This close.

SAM. So?

RICK. So we both know you can figure this one. But you're just giving up, aren't you? Kissing this one off?

SAM. When I get back to New York I'll be kissing my detective badge good-bye, thanks to my lovely visit to Mustique.

RICK. If you're a failure it's because you let yourself become one. After all, it's a hell of a lot easier settling for failure, certainly a lot less work and it definitely takes the least talent. But maybe you really are so dumb that you don't know what Steinberg getting plowed at pointblank range means!

SAM. *(loud, getting mad)* It means Steinberg knew his killer. Is that what you wanted me to say?

RICK. *(louder back)* No kidding? Is that all you can come up with?

SAM. *(louder, barking back)* It means Steinberg wasn't in fear of his killer, otherwise he would never have let his guard down and allowed them to get this close.

RICK. *(soft)* Point, Detective Lyric.

RIGFIELD. So –

*(Everyone looks at **RIGFIELD** to complete the thought. He thinks for a moment.)*

RIGFIELD. – So probably it wasn't someone after the submarine, because Steinberg was guarding the chart at the time.

RICK. Point, Inspector Rigfield. So what do we have left?

RIGFIELD. Someone who had a personal grudge against Steinberg?

RICK. Inspector Rigfield takes the lead.

RIGFIELD. Except that doesn't narrow it down all that much.

RICK. But not just anyone with a grudge against Steinberg. Remember your pointblank range! Someone who he knew and didn't fear as well. Right, Detective Lyric? You know exactly where I'm leading with this, don't you?

SAM. Maybe.

*(**SAM** gets ready to drink again, but **RICK** puts his hand over the glass.)*

RICK. Finish it, and I don't mean the drink.

SAM. Steinberg was killed by someone who wanted to settle the score.

(He looks at **SHEILA.** *So does* **RIGFIELD** *and everyone else.)*

SHEILA. Why is everyone looking at me?

RICK. Because you're the image of the first half of that score. Steinberg was only the second half.

SAM. Tonight someone asked me what do you do when someone kills the only thing in the whole world you really love. I said cry or get even. I didn't expect her to do both. You said your husband was named Sam – Samuel Rocco, wasn't it? The man Steinberg hired Maureen to kill.

SYDNEY. Yes.

SAM. You gave yourself away when you handed over that gray envelope of $10,000.

RICK. The same gray enevlope Steinberg handed Maureen before she was killed.

SAM. I'm sorry, Sydney.

*(***SYNDEY*** *pulls out a .32 gun.)*

SYDNEY. There's nothing to be sorry about, Sam. I had to do it. I don't expect you to understand – so I won't try to explain.

(She turns to leave, but **RIGFIELD** *is blocking the exit.)*

SAM. Just drop the gun, Sydney. You'll never get away with it.

SYDNEY. Of course not. If the owner of a supper club could figure it out – don't you think Steinberg's associates could, too? And they have a longer reach.

*(***RIGFIELD*** *starts for her, but she turns and aims her gun at him.* **SAM** *grabs the gun left behind the bar and aims it at* **SYDNEY***.)*

SAM. Please, Sydney.

SYDNEY. I'm counting on you, Sam!

(There's a tense pause. Slowly **SAM** *lowers the gun.)*

RICK. Oh no!

> (**SYDNEY** *turns the gun into her chest.* **SHEILA** *is the closest to her, so she struggles with her over the gun.*)

SYDNEY. Let go of my gun!

SHEILA. Are you kidding? It's a bitch getting blood out of the carpet.

> (**RICK** *joins the struggle. He is followed by* **SAM** *and then* **RIGFIELD**, *who all struggle over the gun. They pause, with the gun held up high by everyone, above their heads.*)

SHEILA. Men! They'll do anything to jump a dame.

SYDNEY. LET GO!

> (*The gun comes down to between everyone, then goes off. Blackout. Spotlight comes up on* **RICK**, *with a drink in hand.*)

RICK. So that's the story. I wouldn't say that when Sam Lyric left Mustique we were the best of friends. But we have kept in touch through postcards. The last one mentioned that he started both a new job as a detective in some small town up in Connecticut, and a trial reconciliation with his wife. St. Vincent's prison is on its own islet and I hear Sydney has been teaching the other inmates and the parrots to sing duets. The parrots sing the lead. The doctors at Kingstown Hospital say after the reconstructive surgery is complete, Rigfield might actually be able to have children someday. Cairo lucked out by only having to turn evidence against the Steinberg gang, who were all extradited back to Key Largo. And Jean has been collecting investors in her ERR Recovery Incorporated. As a matter of fact, I even put in a few thousand. You see, when Steinberg went overboard, he dropped the mortgage for the Cafe Noir, which Sheila and I found, along with the 20 portraits of Madison from the Baccarat game. I guess it all goes to show that you really do have to put up with a lot of bad turns before a good one comes your way. But if that wasn't the case, wouldn't life be boring?

(There is the sound of a gunshot off stage.)

SHEILA. *(off stage)* OH RICK!

RICK. That's something we never seem to have to worry about down here, at the Cafe Noir.

(He toasts the crowd. Blackout. Curtain call. Prizes are awarded.)

THE END

APPENDIX

The following is an example of the wrap-up:

RICK. For those of you who still haven't figured it out, Sydney killed them all to get revenge for the murder of her husband in New York.

SHELIA. The movie that inspired this play was the 1948 Humphrey Bogart/Lauren Becall classic *Key Largo*, also starring Edward G Robinson as Johnny Rocco, Lionel Barrymore as James Temple and Claire Trevor as Gray Dawn. The film was directed by John Houston.

RICK. Now let's see how many winners we have tonight – so when we call your name, if you'll just wave so we can honor you – *(read names)*.

(All the correct answers are placed in a hat and a character draws the prize winner.)

RICK. Mr. Cairo, tell them what they've won!

(SHEILA models the mug as CAIRO describes it.)

CAIRO. You've won a beautiful, 10 oz. ceramic MURDER TO GO coffee mug, which you can use to impress your friends and work colleagues.

(SHEILA or RICK presents the mug to the winner.)

RICK. We hope you enjoyed the evening and Thank you again for coming to the Cafe Noir. Good night and drive safely.

MOB SILENCES SQUEALERS

New York – The mob bust of the century is turning into a bust itself. New York City's harbor commissioner Samuel Rocco was shot dead yesterday outside his Brooklyn Heights apartment. Mr. Rocco was under police protection and had agreed to turn evidence against his gangster associates in a plea bargain for a lighter sentence. But yesterday the name of Samuel Rocco was added to a growing list of mob informers to fall prey to an assassins bullet. Rocco was supposedly going to give testimony that would link smuggling operations here in the Grenadines with New York mobsters. How deeply the crime element here is involved in the recent crack down in New York is still a mystery.

MUSTIQUE ISLAND CELEBRATES 300 YEARS

The three hundredth birthday of Mustique island's colonization is being celebrated at the Cafe Noir with an exhibit depicting the islands unique history. The rare photos and prints have been painstakingly collected by Mr. Richard Archer, the co-manager of the cafe. He has entitled the exhibit "300 Years of Shady Business." Locals and tourist alike will find the exhibit informing and entertaining.

Works by
David Landau...

The Altos

Bullets for Broadway

Contempt of Court

Murder at Cafe Noir

Murderous Crossing

Noir Pointblank

Noir Suspicions

Please visit our website **samuelfrench.com** for complete
descriptions and licensing information.

OTHER TITLES AVAILABLE FROM SAMUEL FRENCH

BULLETS FOR BROADWAY

Book & Lyrics by David Landau
Music by Killer Tracks

Interactive Mystery / 3m, 3f

A sequel to *The Altos*, Tony & Toffee Alto are back, by popular demand. This time, Toffee wants to be a Broadway star and Tony needs to "clean" some money. So he hires two producers to mount a hit musical - "The Mafia Queen" - starring Toffee. The only catch - the show must be sold out opening night and get great reviews, no matter what it costs - or else! Leave it to Baxter Mallystock and his playwright partner Eli Blain. You're invited to the party after opening night to revile as the reviews come in, along with the FBI and a few stray bullets. It's a brand new evening of Mystery, Comedy, Music and great Food which just goes to prove that sometimes when people say they're going to make a hit, they mean it!

OTHER TITLES AVAILABLE FROM SAMUEL FRENCH

MURDER AT CAFE NOIR

David Landau
Music and Lyrics by Nikki Stern

Mystery / 4m, 3f / Interior

The most popular mystery dinner show in the country, *Murder at Cafe Noir* has enjoyed weekly productions coast to coast since its premiere in 1989. This forties detective story come to life features Rick Archer, P.I., out to find a curvaceous runaway on the forgotten island of Mustique, a place stuck in a black and white era. The owner of the Cafe Noir has washed ashore, murdered, and Rick's quarry was the last person seen with him. He employs his hard boiled talents to find the killer. Was it the French madame and club manager, the voodoo priestess, the shyster British attorney, the black marketeer or the femme fatale? The audience votes twice on what they want Rick to do next and these decisions change the flow of this comic tribute to the Bogart era.

"Mystery theatre at its finest."
– Sun Times, Portland

"Aptly tongue in check [with] clever punch lines and occasional song interludes."
– Washington Times

"Fast and funny satire."
– L.A. Times

"This whodunit is darn good it's the kind of show that lingers on you mind, like a dame's perfume."
– Maryland Journal

"A feast for connoisseurs of mystery."
– Orange County Daily Pilot

SAMUELFRENCH.COM

OTHER TITLES AVAILABLE FROM SAMUEL FRENCH

NOIR SUSPICIONS

David Landau
Music and Lyrics by Nikki Stern

Mystery / 4m, 3f

In this hard boiled comic mystery sequel to the ever-popular *Murder at Cafe Noir*, ex-private eye Rick Archer is now the confused manager of Cafe Noir on the island of Mustique. He is confronted with a corpse on the dock, a mysterious femme fatale, a French blackmailer and a businessman who wants both the cafe and the woman. Rick is arrested after the blackmailer is murdered in his club. It is up to the audience to convince the magistrate that he is innocent. A tribute to *Casablanca* with many references to the classic movie, *Noir Suspicions* is guaranteed to delight audiences whether or not they are familiar with *Murder at Cafe Noir.*

"Embroiling."
– *The New York Times*

"Blockbuster evening [of] great theater."
– *Parsippany News*

"Good fun, good taste."
– *Forbes*

"Exceptional."
– WOR-Radio